Helena Pielichaty (pronounced Pierre-li-hatty) has written numerous books for children, including *Simone's Letters*, which was nominated for the Carnegie Medal. Football has often been a theme in Helena's writing, beginning with *There's Only One Danny Ogle* (OUP 2000) about a boy who happens to support Helena's favourite club, Huddersfield Town. Helena is a fan of the women's game, too, influenced no doubt by her Auntie Pat playing for Yorkshire Copperworks in the 1950s. Her daughter also played for various teams from the age of 10 onwards. The Griffins U11s, a local girls' team, inspired many of the stories in Girls FC.

Is An Own Goal Bad?

Helena Pielichaty

WALKER
BOOKS

For the mighty Lincoln Griffins U11 Lionesses and Eagles – thank you for making my Saturday mornings so tense and exciting!

First published 2009 by Walker Books Ltd
This edition published 2018
87 Vauxhall Walk, London SE11 5HJ

10 9 8 7 6 5 4 3 2 1

This book has been typeset in Helvetica and Handwriter

Printed and bound in Great Britain by CPI Group (UK) Ltd

British Library Cataloguing in Publication Data:
a catalogue record for this book is available from the British Library

ISBN 978-1-4063-8344-7

www.walker.co.uk

MIX
Paper from
responsible sources
FSC
www.fsc.org   FSC® C020471

The Team

⚽ **Megan "Meggo" Fawcett** GOAL

⚽ **Petra "Wardy" Ward** DEFENCE

⚽ **Lucy "Goose" Skidmore** DEFENCE

⚽ **Dylan "Dyl" or "Psycho 1" McNeil** LEFT WING

⚽ **Holly "Hols" or "Wonder" Woolcock** DEFENCE

⚽ **Veronika "Nika" Kozak** MIDFIELD

⚽ **Jenny-Jane "JJ" or "Hoggy" Bayliss** MIDFIELD

⚽ **Gemma "Hursty" or "Mod" Hurst** MIDFIELD

⚽ **Eve "Akka" Akboh** STRIKER

⚽ **Tabinda "Tabby" or "Tabs" Shah** STRIKER/MIDFIELD

⚽ **Daisy "Dayz" or "Psycho 2" McNeil** RIGHT WING

⚽ **Amy "Minto" or "Lil Posh" Minter** VARIOUS

Official name: Parrs Under 11s, also known as the Parsnips

Ground: Lornton FC, Low Road, Lornton

Capacity: 500

Affiliated to: the Nettie Honeyball Women's League
junior division

Sponsors: Sweet Peas Garden Centre, Mowborough

Club colours: red and white; red shirts with white sleeves,
white shorts, red socks with white trim

Coach: Hannah Preston

Assistant coach: Katie Regan

Pre-match Interview

Hello, person reading this!! We are Daisy and Dylan McNeil. We are identical twins. We play football for the Parrs Under 11s. We're the smallest and youngest on the team. (We begin a lot of sentences with "we"!)

Our glorious captain, Megan, has let us write about the Nettie Honeyball Cup run. Have you ever seen a cup run? We haven't, but we have seen one fall. He! He! (If you are a top banana you would smile at that. If you are not a top banana, like our teacher Miss Parkinson, you will have pulled a sour face and thought something like "Girls! Just for once, is it too much to ask that you concentrate on the task you have been set?" We know you are a top banana, person reading this, otherwise you wouldn't have chosen a book about

girls' football, would you? You'd
choose one on verrucas or something.)

By the way, if you saw what Lucy
Skidmore put at the end of her story,
about us writing ours upside-down or
in Elvish, don't worry. Although we
did try writing upside-down — because
we thought it might be fun — it just
gave us a headache. And we don't even
like Elvish. We think he was a rubbish
singer. No, we have written our
story in a traditional way, like the
highly good but dead author Mrs Enid
Blyton would have. We've used chapter
headings and had it spell-checked and
everything.

Yours divinely,
Daisy and Dylan McNeil

1

*In which **Miss Dylan McNeil** writes about the first match in the Nettie Honeyball Cup, using her best vocabulary (not always found in ordinary dictionaries)*

Our story begins once upon a time on the last Saturday of the October half-term holiday. I was trying to have a deep slumber, because I knew on Monday I would have to get up early and face the cruel and cold weather as well as the cruel and cold Miss Parkinson. The trouble was I could not slumber in a deep manner because I could hear the phone ringing. I waited, thinking someone would get it, but nobody did. "Don't worry, I'll go," I said to my twin sister, who didn't move a smidgen. Daisy could sleep through a hurricane, lucky thing.

So I slipped into my slipperoos and went to answer the phone. This takes a while when you live in a windmill and your bedroom is on the top floor and the phone is in the kitchen on the bottom floor. Usually, by the time you have travelled all the way down all the spiral staircases, past your parents' bedroom on one floor and your twin brothers' bedroom on the next floor and your living room with all your mum's paintings on the floor beneath that and then landed in the kitchen, the phone has stopped ringing and all you can do is sigh and pat Sedge, your beloved border collie, then go back upstairs. Today, though, the phone didn't stop ringing. So I answered it, hoping Sedge wouldn't mind waiting for his pat.

"Hello, may I help you?" I asked in a highly polite way, in case it was someone wanting to buy one of Mummy's paintings.

"Who's that?" a sharp voice at the other end replied.

"Felicity Wishes," I answered, because everyone

10

knows it's silly to tell strangers your real name on the phone.

The stranger sighed. "Dylan or Daisy?" she asked.

"It might be," I said.

"Daisy, it's your Granny Susan!"

Then I knew it really was because I recognized her voice, even though it was coming all the way from Scotland. "Oh, Granny. Och aye the noo!"

She tutted. "Och! How many times do I have to tell you, nobody says 'Och aye the noo.' Not in Dundee, anyhow."

"Not even the Loch Ness Monster?"

"Daisy, do you know what time it is?"

"Actually, I'm Dylan. You can tell us apart because I don't nibble my nailies."

"Dylan, do you know what time it is?"

"I do chew my hair locks, though. It's a filthy habit."

"Dylan, listen to me. Do you know what time it is?"

"Nope."

"It's half-past nine."

"OK. Well, thanks for letting me know. That's very kind of you. Now, about the Loch Ness Monster … did it ever have babies?"

"Dylan, you've remembered you've got a football match at half-past ten this morning, haven't you?"

I frowned. I hadn't. I squinnied across at the back door. The back door has a big nail and a little nail thumped into it. On the big nail we keep the calendar and on the little nail we keep our fixture list. Both were missing. "Oops," I said.

"Tch! I knew it! It's a good job I've got a copy of your list or you'd all be up the Swanee without a paddle. Away now and get ready."

"Er … Granny…?"

"Greenbow Community Centre."

"Thank you."

"It's the cup match against Greenbow United Girls."

"Oh! A cup match! Guess what? Megan wants me and Daisy to write up all about the cup matches."

"Well you'd better get a move on, or there'll be nothing to write about!" she said and hung up.

Of course it was all go, go, go after that! We must not miss the first match of the cup run. We must not! I ran back up the stairs and shouted into my mum and dad's room, "Wake up, Snoozeheads! It's football!" and then I ran to my brothers Declan and Darwin's room and shouted, "Wake up, Snorybrains! It's football!" but when I ran to my bedroom I didn't shout. I shook Daisy awake and said, "Twinny! It's footy and I'm not even fibbing!" and Daisy scowled and said, "When?" and I said, "In, like, an hour" and she said, "Oh no!"

Do you know what, though, person reading this? We were all ready and climbing into Chutney, our faithful camper van, by ten past ten. That is a McNeil McRecord, that is.

At first Daisy and me were really excited and we talked about the match. "Do you think they'll wear green bows?" I asked her, and she said, "They might – but the Grove Belles didn't wear bells, remember?" I nodded, because it was sad but true. Then we chatted some more about playing and I got that twingly-wooshy feeling in my tummy because I wanted to get out on that field and run like a champion. "Are we there yet?" I asked Jim, our beloved bearded father.

"No, Greenbow's out towards Leicester; we'll be another half-hour at least," he replied.

Daisy stopped talking in an instant when she heard that mood-damping news, and she just stared out of the window when I tried more chit-chat, so in the end I helped Darwin with his knitting instead. Have I mentioned that Darwin is an excellent knitter? He can knit you anything as long as it's something long and thin. I have put in a request for mittens for kittens when he is more experienced. Declan, on the other hand, is not a knitter. He prefers projects involving sawing and hammering and a hint of danger. Building things and falling out of our treehouse are his specialities.

Eventually, after ages and ages, and miles and

miles, we found the Greenbow estate, but we couldn't find the community centre because every street we went down seemed to be a dead end full of cars on bricks. "It's badly signposted," Dad said, as he reversed Chutney into a pub car park sprinkled with pretty sparkly glass.

We finally arrived just as it began to frizz with rain. "It's a good thing we've brought our cagoules," I said to Daisy. "Do you think Hannah will let us wear them to play in?" Daisy didn't reply. Her eyelashes were pressed against the window. "Daisy, I said it's a good thing we've brought our cagoules," I repeated.

"I'd leave Daisy alone," Darwin told me. "She's upset."

When I looked closely at her, I could tell he was right. Her face was blubby. "Let's do the jolly football clapping song!" I said in a highly encouraging voice. I held my hands out, ready. "Come on! 'Two-four-six-eight, who do we appreciate...' Your turn, Daisy!"

I paused and waited. The next lines were "Not

the King, not the Queen, but the Parsnips football team" – but Daisy was not interested.

"There's no point," she replied.

"Of course there is!" Luna, our beloved spiky-pink-haired mother, encouraged. "If you hurry you might get five minutes."

"We won't," Daisy said. "They've finished. Look!"

My heart sank then. What Daisy had said was true. Coming towards us, in small grouplets of two and three, were our teamies.

At the front was Megan, our brave and honest ball-stopper captain, and her best friends Petra and the scrunch-faced Jenny-Jane. They had their arms round each other and looked victorious. Near by, Tabinda was waving her shinglepads at her father and chatting, and on the other side of them Lucy Skidmore and Holly Woolcock were laughing. I couldn't tell who else was approaching the car park as they were still too far away.

"Let's go," Daisy said, her voice full of urgency. "Let's go before they see us."

"Are you sure?" Dad asked. "Don't you want to explain what happened? Or see how it went?"

"No," Daisy replied in a mope-laden voice.

Dad twisted round and glanced at me. I shook my head. My twin was right. The match was over, so we should simply return home without further ado.

As Dad started Chutney's engine, Mum leaned over and patted Daisy on her knee. "Sorry, my love. It was worth a try, though, eh?"

"Not really," Daisy muttered, ducking down and unscrabbling her laces.

I chewed my lip and hoped my twin wasn't going to be in a skulk for the rest of the weekend. It does grate on my gums when she skulks.

Anyway, we returned to our beloved windmill on Windmill Lane, had breakfast and fed the precious and beloved dog, hens, rabbits, guinea pigs and cats – but not the fox, because he is wild and gets his own nibbles.

2

*In which **Daisy McNeil** explains to Megan Fawcett*

why the twins missed the first match of the

Nettie Honeyball Cup

**On Monday morning I went to school
feeling that my chest was being squashed
by a giant's foot.** I was so nervous. What was I
going to tell Megan? She would not be very pleased
with us, especially as we had promised her we'd
make a good job of writing up the reports. "Are you
sure you can deliver?" she had asked.

"Oh yes!" we'd said together. "We'll be highly
excellent. We've got really remarkable reading
ages and vocabularies for our year. Ask
anyone."

"Though our spelling's a challenge," I warned.

"Go on, then," Megan had agreed.

And now we'd messed up already and she was going to be so disappointed.

Luckily, when we got to school, Megan and Petra happened to be the greeters on door duty. Greeters miss lessons for a whole day and get to ask people to sign in, and then they escort them to Mr Glasshouse or the staffroom and such things. This is to show how kind and polite pupils at Mowborough Primary School are, and to make visitors feel welcome. Dylan and me cannot wait to be greeters. We'll be so sublime at it.

Anyway, Megan and Petra being the greeters meant I didn't even have to wait until break to get the giant's foot off my chest. I could go straight away, though I would have to do it without telling Miss Parkinson. Miss Parkinson is not good at understanding things like giants' feet on your chest, so there was no point telling her.

As soon as Miss Parkinson had her back to me, I slid out of my place. Dylan was on the other side of the classroom plaiting her friend Ellie's hair and did not see me sliding, thank goodness. It was better if I did this on my own.

My knees were a little on the shaky side when I approached the greeters' table. "Hello, Meganini." I smiled, pretending to be all breezy. "Hello, Petrasaurus."

"Hello, Dayz," they chirped. They didn't sound angry at all! Hurrah!

"Erm ... how is the greeting going?"

"So-so." Megan shrugged. "A bit boring, really."

I glanced at the visitors' signing-in book. The page was bare.

"Is there anything we can do for you, Daisy?" Petra asked.

I took in the deepest of breaths in case they secretly *were* cross but were hiding it well. "It's about the cup match."

"Uh-huh."

"We missed it."

"We know. Don't worry about it," Megan said before I could explain.

I blinked. Don't worry about it? How kind! Often when we miss things people get cross or say something like "Typical" or "I might have known you would." Unless it's the dentist – then we just pay a fine.

"It's a pity you missed the game. It was a cracker! We won three–one!" Petra added. Her grin was as wide as a watermelon.

"So what should we do about writing up the match? Should we just make something up?" I asked.

Megan shook her head. "Don't worry about it. Hannah's already posted her match report on the website, so we have a record; that's the main thing."

"Oh. I didn't know Hannah did that."

"Yes. She always writes the match reports. She does ours and the Parrs'."

"Oh."

"Just print that out."

"OK."

"Print out the table, too. It shows where we are in the group."

"Is that important?" I asked. Tables sounded too mathsy to me. Maths is not one of my best subjects. Ask Miss Parkinson.

Megan nodded. "Not half! Only the top team in each of the two groups goes through to the final."

"Really?"

"Yep. Basically, we've got to win every match we play in the cup run. Our position is everything."

"Lucky for us the Grove Belles and the Tembridge Vixens are in Group B," Petra added.

"That's good?" I said, as it seemed expected.

"Good? It's brilliant!" Petra laughed. "It means one of the best two teams will have to knock the other out to reach the final. We could go all the way in our group!"

"Oh! I'll tell all this to Dylan!"

Megan nodded. "You do that."

"I shall."

There was a short silence. "I'd do it now, before you forget," Megan urged.

"I shall. Erm … you know the printing thing?"

"Uh-huh?"

"Do you need a computer for that?"

"Yes."

"It's just we don't have one at home." (We don't have a TV, either, but when you tell people that they think you're weird, and I was already in deep mud so I just left it at no computer for now.)

Megan shrugged. "No worries. I'll do it at lunchtime for you."

Megan was being kind again! No wonder she's our captain.

I returned to the classroom without a giant's foot on my chest. Not even a giant's toe. I was so happy that I wouldn't have cared if Miss Parkinson had yelled her head off at me – but she was already yelling at Callum Kirton so I was able to sneak back to my seat. Callum Kirton is the most naughty boy in our class. Dylan loves him and says she's going to marry him after she has travelled the world in a hot-air balloon.

At lunchtime, just as she'd promised, Megan gave me the report, the table and even a new fixture list.

Here is the match report:

NETTIE HONEYBALL CUP
Group A

Parrs U11s (Parsnips) 3
Greenbow United Girls 1

Saturday 27 October

What an awesome way to start our cup run! Defending in the first half were Lucy Skidmore and Holly Woolcock. Both were brilliant at keeping a determined Greenbow at bay. Gemma had a couple of shots on target and was unlucky not to score, but she set up two for super-striker Eve Akboh.

In the second half Greenbow put us under pressure. They came out all guns blazing and deserved their goal, which came ten minutes into the half from a sharply headed cross. By now the match had a real buzz about it and Greenbow almost equalized in a classic goalmouth scramble, but life-saver Holly cleared off the line. Nika then broke free and took the ball forward, passing unselfishly to Tabinda, who powered home goal number three. Well done, Tabinda!

Parsnip of the Match went to Gemma Hurst for being outstanding (again).

Hannah Preston (coach)

☆ **Next cup match: Saturday 15 December at HOME against Lutton Ash; 10.30 KO**

"Oh," I said when I read it, "so Gemma won the golden globey?"

"The what?"

"The Parsnip of the Match."

"Yes – she played a blinder."

"That's good," I said, swallowing hard, "that's very good."

"Check out who's top of the table!" Megan said, tapping the second sheet.

This was the second sheet:

Team	P	W	D	L	F	A	Pts
Parrs U11s	1	1	0	0	3	1	3
Lutton Ash Angels	1	0	1	0	2	2	1
Misslecott Goldstars	1	0	1	0	2	2	1
Greenbow United Girls	1	0	0	1	1	3	0
Furnston Diamonds	0	0	0	0	0	0	0

"Us!" I grinned.

"It won't last, but it's nice to be top for even a little while. Furnston haven't played yet, that's why they don't have any points," Megan explained. "We all miss a go. Actually, it's our turn to miss next. We don't play a cup match again until December the fifteenth."

"December the fifteenth! That's a long time away."

"Yep. So you've nothing to do until then."

"No," I said, feeling a bit sad about that, "unless

you want me to write up about one of the league matches…"

"No, you're fine," Megan said quickly. "Just concentrate on the cup."

"Okey-dokey," I said. "I'll do that … we both will. Cross my heart hope to die put a needle in my eye."

"No needles needed – just be there."

"That's a promise, captain," I told her and saluted.

3

*The report of the Nettie Honeyball Cup football match between the Parrs Under 11s and Lutton Ash Angels as told by **Miss Dylan McNeil***

This next bit begins once upon a time on the morning of Saturday 15 December.

I was trying to have a deep slumber because it was only nine days to Christmas and I knew I wouldn't be getting much slumber soon what with Yuletide excitement. Only the phone was ringing and ringing and my slumber was disappearing and disappearing. "That's fine, I'll go," I muttered to Daisy.

As I may have mentioned last time, person reading this, answering the phone is not easy when you live in a windmill and your bedroom is on the top floor and the phone is on the bottom floor.

It is even harder at Christmas-time when it is freezing cold and your beloved mother has wrapped tinsel round all the spiral-staircase handrails.

This time when I reached the kitchen the phone had stopped – but only because Daisy had answered it. "Yes, Grandma," she was saying, "I know. Thank you."

"Huh? I thought you were in bed!" I told Daisy when she hung up.

"I thought *you* were going to wake me up for the match!" she told me as she dashed past.

Of course it was all go, go, go after that! We must not miss the second match of the cup run. We must not! I ran back up the stairs and shouted into my mum and dad's room, "Wake up! Football!" and then I ran to my brothers' room and shouted, "Wake up! Football!" but when I ran to our bedroom I didn't shout anything to Daisy. I didn't need to because she was already up. Not only that – she was out of her jimjameroos and in her kit. "Crikey!" I said. "That was quick!"

"Hurry up!" Daisy said, shooing my cat Pickle off my bed and pulling my kit out from beneath her. "We mustn't be late. I promised Megan."

"Did you cross your heart and hope to die?"

"Yep."

"Gosh! Let's go, then!"

At least this time we were playing at Lornton, which is only two villages and a wiggly bit away.

"Who are we up against this morn?" I asked, eating toast and pulling my hoodie on at the same time, as we walked to the van.

"Lutton Ash Angels," she said.

I stopped dead, right there and then, on the frosty pathway. "Angels?"

"Not real angels," Daisy said and pushed me into Declan, who was climbing into Chutney.

"Watch it!" he growled.

Mum yawned and closed the door, then climbed onto the front passenger seat next to Dad. "I can't believe we're doing this. It's madness," she said. "Why can't football just be played in summer?"

"Please hurry, Dad," Daisy said. "It's ten o'clock. The match starts at half-past."

"We're playing angels," I told him.

"OK, OK, don't rush me. I don't like being rushed," Dad said, and started the engine. "Rushing makes me stressed."

"It's not helping Chutney much either," Declan said.

It was true. Chutney wasn't sounding tip-top. More tip-bottom.

"Yep. She's struggling," Dad said, turning the key again. "Oh dear. I've flooded the engine now."

"Oh no!" Daisy exclaimed.

"Here we go," Darwin muttered and got out his knitting.

"We'll just have to sit and wait a while," Dad said.

"Why now?" Daisy moaned. "Why can't she conk out on school days instead?"

"I can guarantee she will." Mum laughed and ruffled Daisy's hair.

"I know! I'll go and get a clippyboard and pen

to write the match description down!" I said and clattered back into the house. I couldn't find a clippyboard but I found an old ringo-binder of Declan's under Sedge's basket and used that.

Did Daisy congratulate me on my fine thinking when I returned to the steamed-up van? No, she did not, person reading this. She did not!

After about ten minutes Dad tried again, but still Chutney would not start. She is not a wet-and-damp-morning-liking kind of vehicle.

"Everybody out! The old girl needs a push," Dad said. After we'd all got out and given Chutney a big push down the slope, she roared into action. When I say roared, I mean chugged.

"Megan's not going to be kind about us being late again like she was before," Daisy skulked as we pulled into Lornton FC's ground.

"But we missed the last game altogether. We're here for loads of it this time," I said.

Daisy tapped her watch three times with her nibbly nail. "Dylan, it's nearly half-time."

"Well, if the matches were the same length as in the men's game it wouldn't matter so much," Dad argued. I could tell from his tone he was getting as fed up with his daughter moaning as I was.

"An hour's long enough, thank you," Mum told him, "and if Megan says anything to either of you, just tell her what happened. We can't help it if the car won't start. That's life."

"Exactly," I said.

The match was in full bellow, with girls running everywhere. The angels were wearing white tops with dark blue shorts and blue and white stripy socks, which I thought was a delightful choice. I went to stand with Daisy and Eve. "Hello, Eve," I said. "How are you?"

"Cold," she replied and began jumping up and down on the spot.

"I'll write that down," I said.

Daisy sighed. "You're supposed to be writing down what happens on the field."

"I know."

"Turn round, then!"

Person reading this, I have to tell you I was getting highly flip-flapped about being bossed around by my sister. After all, I am three and a half minutes older than her and she has no right to be grating on my gums.

I turned round very, very slowly, as if in a dream or a mime. Eve gave me an odd little look but I didn't care. On the field there was much shouting, a highly lot of it coming from Hannah. "Move to the ball a bit more, Nika!" "Who's on number 15?" "Lovely pass, JJ! Keep going!"

I had just written the word "Move" when Tabinda came racing towards us.

"Uh-oh, this doesn't look good," Eve said, and jumped aside just as Tabinda doubled over and was sick.

"Do you think I should describe that?" I asked Daisy.

Daisy shook her head. "Mrs Enid Blyton would

never describe puke," she said in a wise manner.

"True. I'll miss that bit out."

Luckily then the stoppy-starter blew her whistle and it was break time, so Tabinda's mum and dad could take her home and I could mingle with my teamies and catch up on the latest news. They all seemed quite skulky and were doing a heap of complaining. "Did you see that one with the dark hair? She fouls all the time!" Gemma said.

"The ref's not even doing anything. Their striker keeps standing on my foot every time I try to throw the ball out!" Megan added.

"Ignore it," Hannah told everybody. "You have to rise above it in matches like this. We're two–one up and there's no reason you can't make that more if you just keep doing what you're doing. OK, get ready, er ... Dyl. I want you on for Tabs."

"I can't," I said. "I'm writing."

"I'll do the writing," Daisy said – and snatched the ringo-binder right out of my hand!

"No, I need you too, Dayz. The field's very muddy;

it's heavy on everybody's legs. I want to swap you in and out."

There was nothing for it but for us both to remove our cagoules, fleeces, outer polo-neck jumpers and gloves.

"Nice and quick," Hannah urged. "I want you left midfield."

"OK, boss," I said and stuck my thumbs up at her.

I have to be honest. When people say things like "left midfield" I get a bit confused. I'm not splendid at left and right or mid or field – so I used my common sense and went to find a space no one else was using, like Miss Parkinson tells us to do in PE. This time I chose a spot quite close to the corner stick, but Megan called out, "No, Dylan, not there. Over there – alongside Hursty." So I darted like a young guppy over to Gemma Hursty and said, "Hello, partner," and she sighed and said, "Move further along the line, Dylan."

Inside my head I thought, well, I don't know where I'm supposed to be, but outside my head I kept quiet because I didn't want Gemma to know that.

Instead I stared at the girl on the opposite side of the white line. I have to admit I was disappointed. She did not look like an angel. Her face was not endearing in the least. In fact, number 5 was what my friend Ellie would call a bit of an Ugly Betty.

The whistle blew and it was our turn with the ball in the middle, and Gemma Hursty passed it to Jenny-Jane and Jenny-Jane did her churny face as she ran, and I had to smile as I ran alongside her because her churny face always makes me smile. Jenny-Jane kicked the ball back to Gemma, even though I was free and available – but that didn't matter because Gemma Hursty ran and ran, dodging and swerving and echoing round the angels until she was near the goalhouse. She then kicked the ball to Nika, who turned and skiddled it past their ball-stopper girl and into the net.

"Goal!" I yelled, and ran like an aeroplane, which is the way I have chosen to celebrate when we score. I zoomed straight over to Daisy for a high five and then zoomed back to my place next to the number 5 angel. "Wasn't that a highly elegant goal?" I asked her.

She pulled a face at me and muttered under her breath two words that my beloved parents have told me I must never use and even my future husband, Callum Kirton, only uses sparingly.

"If you use those words again I shall report you to the stoppy-starter," I told her in a firm manner.

I am not going to tell you what happened during the rest of the match, person reading this, because it will spoil it for you when you read my splendid and excellent report. Let's just say we were victorious.

4

*In which **Daisy McNeil** describes how Dylan suffers
a set-back and Daisy learns a lot*

**"Why won't you let me see it?" I said to
Dylan the Monday after the match.**

I hurried after her as she marched into the dining
room.

"Because," Dylan said, clutching the report to
her chest.

"Because what?"

"Because blot."

We reached the Year Four table. Megan was
sitting with Petra and Tabinda. Megan was eating a
tuna-and-salad sandwich, and Petra was scraping
the inside of a raspberry-yoghurt pot, and Tabinda

was shaking a carton of apple juice and seeing if there was anything left.

"Hello, teamies," Dylan announced.

The three of them looked up at us. "Hello, twins," Megan said.

"I bring you gold, frankincense and lemonade," Dylan said and threw down her report. It landed in Petra's sandwich box.

"Nice wrapping," Petra said, handing the brown envelope covered in red glitter and tinsel cuttings back to Dylan.

"No, it's for Meganini – it's the match report," Dylan told her.

Megan scowled. "But you only came for the second half."

"Don't worry, I covered the first half using my imagination," Dylan said. "Pages one to six. No probs."

Petra put her hand over her mouth and looked quickly away. I thought she was going to laugh, but she didn't. Instead she began to clear away all the lunch stuff. "We'll leave you to it, Megs," she said.

"Thanks, ex-friends," Megan replied.

"It's a mighty piece of writing," Dylan told Megan. "Even Miss Parkinson would give it three stickers, probably."

Megan took a deep breath and slowly pulled the sheets out of the envelope. I leaned forward, trying to peer over Dylan's shoulder, but she elbowed me out of the way. Charming.

Our captain began to read. As she read, her face turned more and more puzzled. She got as far as the bottom of the first page, then stopped. "Sorry, Dyl, but there's no way," she said.

I took a step back in case Dylan did one of her fainting moves, but she stayed upright. "No way what?" she asked.

"No way we can use that."

"Which bit?"

"Any bit."

"Any? Gosh! Pray why?"

Megan chewed at her lip. "Look, I'm not trying

to be mean or anything. I can tell you've tried hard, but it's really difficult to read and it's too … it's too … um … confusing."

My heart sank then. I had guessed it would be! This was why I'd wanted Dylan to show the report to me first. My spelling's not highly great but Dylan's is dreadful. She spells Dylan D-y-l-n and Daisy D-a-s-e. And that's before we get onto the made-up words. Mr Glasshouse had wanted Mum and Dad to let Dylan be assessed, but Mum had told him "No way" because she didn't want her labelled like a packet of cheese. "It's all schools seem to do these days," Mum said; "run tests and tick boxes so they've got something to show the inspectors. Well, their statistics won't include *my* children!" She got in quite a tizz about it, and said if it wasn't for the fact she needs to paint she'd educate us at home.

"Confusing? Is it? Where?" Dylan asked Megan, snatching the report out of her hands.

"Read a bit out loud to me and I'll tell you," Megan said.

"My pleasure," Dylan replied and, taking a deep breath, she began. "'Well, today, the Parsnips had perfect conditions of rain and churny grass. It was highly glorious. The first thing I noticed was that the lady stoppy-starter had a kind face but lard-laden legs. The second thing I noticed was that the Lutton Ash Angels passed in a speedy way like a moth caught in the sunscreen of a bus driver's window. One of the angels (who wasn't a real angel, by the way) kicked the ball towards the netty-box. Petra, playing at stopper-back, tried to kick it out but she skiddled on the mud and another angel flumped it with her foot straight past Megan, our brave ball-stopper...'"

"Stop!" Megan called out, holding her head.

"But I've only read a slither," Dylan protested.

Megan shook her head. "Dyl, it won't do! You have to use proper words for things. The referee's a referee, not a ... what did you put?"

"A stoppy-starter."

"A stoppy-starter. Exactly. And I'm not a

ball-stopper, I'm a goalkeeper or 'keeper'. Proper words."

"I thought people reading it might be a bit tired of the proper words and like a change. Miss Parkinson is always telling us to broaden our vocabulary. She is, isn't she, Daisy?"

Actually Miss Parkinson's always telling us the same as Megan: to write less and to stop making words up. She goes cross-eyed when we hand things in – but I wasn't going to embarrass my twin by telling Megan that. "She is," I agreed.

Megan shook her head again. "Sorry, guys, but I can't use this. Women who play football for Chelsea or Leicester City Women might read about us one day. You have to keep it real. Have you included the Group A table?"

"No."

"Well, you must. That's vital."

So she took us over to the IT Room and printed out Hannah's official match report and the vital Group A table from the website again, and said

Dylan could decorate them or something.

After Megan had gone, I asked Dylan if she was all right. "Course I'm all right!" she said. "It's not Meganini's fault she's not a good reader like us. She's probably never even heard of Mrs Enid Blyton. I'll keep it shorter next time and write in capitals to help her out." She handed me the report and the table and went off to find Ellie.

Here is the match report written by Hannah:

NETTIE HONEYBALL CUP
Group A

Parrs U11s (Parsnips) 7
Lutton Ash Angels 1

Saturday 15 December

After awful weather all week it looked as if we'd have to postpone the match, but the rain held off long enough for us to go ahead.

This was our first meeting against Lutton Ash Angels. They began sprightly enough and scored after seven minutes while we were still waking up. Luckily Nika equalized from a deft pass by Gemma a minute later. Our midfield did a fantastic job of keeping the ball going forward, and we were rewarded with a second goal just before half-time after a nice one-two between Gemma and JJ, who tapped it in.

In the second half Gemma's incisive runs and even more incisive crosses to Eve up front soon saw us four—one up, with Eve netting one and Nika her second. The fifth, scored by Gemma, deserves a special mention. She swerved round not one, not two, but three Lutton Ash defenders, then nutmegged the keeper to slot home a sweet solo effort even the England Women's manager Hope Powell would have applauded! Lutton Ash's defence could only stand and stare.

Ten minutes before the end, the heavens opened and the field, already muddy, turned into a swamp. This had a negative effect on Lutton Ash. Our last two goals were from penalties. Penalties at this level are rare, so having two awarded shows how bad things got. Well done to our girls for not retaliating and to Amy for scoring her first goal of the season. Way to go, Minto!

Our six points puts us on equal points with Furnston at the top of the table.

Remember, only the top team from each group qualifies for the final. The next one will be a nail-biter — it's against Furnston. Furnston beat the Angels six—one back in November and Misslecott five—nil on Saturday so they're obviously the ones to watch!

Parsnip of the Match: Nika. Awesome, Nika!

Hannah Preston (coach)

☆ **Next cup match: Saturday 9 February at HOME against Furnston; 10.30 KO**

I sighed at the part where Nika won the golden globey, then turned to the table:

Team	P	W	D	L	F	A	Pts
Furnston Diamonds	2	2	0	0	11	1	6
Parrs U11s	2	2	0	0	10	2	6
Misslecott Goldstars	3	0	2	1	5	10	2
Greenbow United Girls	2	0	1	1	4	6	1
Lutton Ash Angels	3	0	1	2	4	15	1

I then folded up the sheets of paper and put them in my bag.

☆ ☆ ☆

When we got home from school we had some surprise news. Granny was coming to stay with us for Christmas. Usually Granny goes on a cruise at Christmas, on a boat called the *Pride of Peebles*, but there was a bug going round so it couldn't sail. "Which means she's coming here," Mum said and scratched the side of her neck. It had a red rash on it. It's called a stress rash and it always comes when Granny visits.

I don't know why Mum gets a stress rash when Granny visits. I think Granny's nice. I like the way she talks and how she phones to make sure we get to things on time. I don't think Mum does, though. She says Gran should realize Jim isn't ten any more and doesn't need her phoning every two minutes to check he's wearing clean underpants.

So anyway, the next few days were really busy because we had the end-of-term Christmas party at school, then we had all the shopping to do and all the logs to chop and all the mince pies and biscuits to bake on top of the usual stuff. And of course there was Santa to think about as well as Granny. I totally forgot about football. I think Dylan did, too. It's only to be expected on special occasions.

Granny arrived on the eve of Christmas Eve at two-thirty in the afternoon, not long after we had got up. "Mum! What a brilliant surprise!" Dad said when he opened the door and saw her there, her dark hair dripping from the rain.

"I'll let you pay for the taxi," she told him before handing Darwin her suitcase.

"Oh, of course," Dad mumbled, and stepped outside in his stripy pyjamas.

"There was no need for you to get a taxi, Sue," Mum told her, standing on tiptoe to kiss her cheek because our granny's very tall. "We could have picked you up."

"Oh? And when might that have been? Hogmanay?" Granny asked. Then she looked round the kitchen, which was perhaps less tidy than it might have been, sighed and said, "A cup of tea would be nice."

"I'll make it," Darwin said immediately. "Peppermint or camomile?"

"Tetley's," Granny replied, and produced a box of tea bags from her handbag.

Then Dad said he'd take Granny's suitcase upstairs, and Mum said she'd come with him to make the bed up. The rash on Mum's neck was so pink it matched her hair.

They were very noisy going up the stairs, with Mum saying, "I thought you said she was coming tomorrow?" and Dad saying, "I thought it was tomorrow, but obviously I was wrong," and Mum saying, "Now she'll think we're as scatterbrained as ever," and Dad saying, "Well, we are as scatterbrained as ever, Luna my love, but does it matter?"

I cleared a space at the table so Granny could sit down.

"Thank you, Dylan," she said.

"I'm Daisy," I told her, and held my fingers out to show her my bitten nails – though to be fair I had been working on my thumbs.

"Hm," she said.

Darwin gave her the tea with the bag still floating on top like a life-jacket.

"Thank you ... er..." She paused. "...Darwin?"

"Well done!" Darwin beamed.

"Two sets of twins, just like I had. What are the chances, eh? But look at the four of you; you've grown so much." She looked pleased then and gave us all a wide smile.

"We're always growing," Declan said, and slid a plate of burnt ginger biscuits we'd made the day before next to the cup.

Granny took one, bit it, grimaced and put the rest of it back down on the plate. "So, tell me all your news."

So we did. All our news. All at once. "Uh-huh, uh-huh, uh-huh," Granny kept saying, her eyes switching from one to the other of us like a crazy metronome. After a bit I stopped talking to give her head a rest and to let Darwin show her his knitting. "Och! That's grand! A man who can knit won't go far wrong in the world," she told him.

I grinned. I liked the way she said "world". It sounded like *wirraled*.

Granny caught me grinning. "And what about you" – she glanced at my nails – "Daisy? How's school?"

"Don't ask!" I told her.

"Is that Miss Parkinson still giving you a hard time over your writing and spelling?"

"Every day."

"Oh dear. Doesn't she help you?"

"Sometimes, but she says until we've had proper tests to see exactly what our problem is there's nothing much she can do about it."

"And we're not having tests because we're not packets of cheese." Dylan sniffed.

"Mum and Dad don't approve of tests," I explained.

Granny nodded. "I know they don't, but a wee one to get you on the right road wouldn't do any harm. After all, not all cheese comes in packets if you shop around," she said mysteriously, then glanced towards the stairs. "But never mind! We'd better not 'go there', had we? I don't want to be in the bad books so soon. How's the football?"

I shrugged. "It's OK."

"OK? Only OK? You've not been made captain yet, then? Either of you?"

Declan snorted. "They'll never be made captain. Not until they learn which end they're playing towards."

Dylan thumped him. "Excuse me! That's highly mean. Mummy's told you on many occasions we aren't allowed to say mean things to each other because it's bad for our self-esteem!"

"You're not allowed to punch, either, Dylan!" Declan said, and thumped her back. Then they began having a bit of a fight.

"Oh, wonderful," Granny said.

"Mind my knitting!" Darwin yelped.

"Shall we go upstairs into the living room?" I said to Granny.

She nodded. "It might be an idea."

The living room was even more untidy than the kitchen. That was because we'd had to move stuff around to make way for the Christmas tree and because none of us had cleared our school things away yet. And because it was never that tidy in the first place, to be honest.

Granny picked her way between backpacks and piles of magazines and books and old beanbags and a few of Mum's canvases before shooing our cats, Beetroot and Pickle, off the settee so she could sit down.

She peered at one of Mum's paintings. It was of a huge bare lady, dancing. "That's *Bella Sings the Blues*," I told her.

"Is it?" she said. "I'm not surprised." She glanced around. "Still no telly, I see?"

"No. It rots the mind."

Granny snorted very loudly. "What nonsense! It's a good job I've brought my laptop so I can watch *Deal or No Deal*, that's all I can say."

"Is that like a computer?"

"It *is* a computer. And a telly. Clever, eh?"

"Can it print things?"

"Only if you've got a printer. Why?"

So I told Granny about the match reports and how we hadn't got one right yet.

"How come?"

"Well, we missed the first match and only got to the second half of the last one. Then—"

"What? You were still late? Even after my phone calls? Och!"

"I know. We all kind of seem ready on time, and then one person goes off to do something and then another one does, and – oh, I don't know…"

"And do people on the team say things when you're late?"

"Sometimes."

"And does it bother you?"

"Yes, because I know if I'm late I'll never win the golden globey..."

"The what?"

"It's a beautiful trophy the best player of the match gets. I..." I paused and listened out in case Dylan or anyone else was around. I had never told anybody this before, but I knew Granny could keep a secret. "I would love to win it – but I know I never will."

"I see." Granny beckoned me closer. "I think it's time you and I had a little chat about tactics, Daisy Nail-biter McNeil."

And that's exactly what we did. We talked tactics, in private, whenever we got the chance between festive mealtimes and present-opening and carol-singing and chocolate-munching and playing Twister. Those discussions were most interesting, I can tell you. I learned a lot.

Granny left the day after Boxing Day. Her train was at twelve, so we had to get up quite early. At eleven-twenty-five Dad tried to reverse Chutney onto the drive, but Chutney wouldn't start. Dad began to apologize to Granny – but as if by magic the taxi she had arrived in swept into our driveway.

"Oh," said Dad. "That's handy."

"That's because I know you like the back of my hand-y, son!" She grinned, and winked at me.

We all waved until she was out of sight – but I stayed there longest because I knew I'd miss her the most.

5

In which **Miss Dylan McNeil** *tells you*

about her terrible mistake

This chapter begins once upon a time on the morning of Saturday 9 February.

I awoke with ringing in my ears, but this time I didn't have to run all the way downstairs because the ringing was actually in my ears, person reading this. *In* my ears! That was because the night before, Daisy had made me sleep with my alarm clock next to my pillow.

Daisy had ringing in her ears, too. Only she had stuck her alarm clock *to* her ears, with sticky plasters, and the clock was hanging from her hair like a monkey from a tree.

"You look funny!" I told her.

"It's worth it," she said, pulling the clock and the plasters off her hair.

Some of the plasters wouldn't come off, so I had to apply scissor usage in the end. I was still a bit sleepy, so some pieces of hair were not straight in the slightest after I'd finished cutting. I frowned. "That's the best I can do, twin sis."

"Och aye the noo, twin sis!"

I looked at her. "You're not skulky with me?"

"No. We're up early. That's all that matters!" she trilled and began pulling her nightie over her head. This next bit I'm going to tell you is strange... Daisy was wearing her football kit already!

"Oh," I said. "I wish I'd thought of that."

"I'm thinking ahead. That's the name of the game."

"Thinking ahead. I might do that from now on." I glanced round. "You don't happen to know where my stuff is, do you?"

"Underneath Beetroot."

"Oh!" I walked over to the old armchair where I read my books and think about important matters and where Beetroot sleeps, said "Excuse me" to the moggle and pulled my shirt from under her. "I can't believe the Furnston people wanted to start the match early. Why can't they have a lie-in? Sleep is precious for children, you know."

"Don't ask me. I only know what Hannah told me last night when she phoned. Do you want to use the bathroom first while I put the kettle on?"

"The kettle?"

"To make Mum and Dad a cup of tea."

"Oh. That's highly kind of you."

"I'm a highly kind girl."

Daisy disappeared then and I decided to sit in my old armchair for a moment or two and stroke Beetroot and think about important things – but just as I'd got to the bit about whether or not I should send Callum Kirton one Valentine card next week or two, Daisy came and dragged me downstairs, saying, "Breakfast's ready."

Downstairs, the whole of my precious family was eating breakfast. "Half-eight," Mother said, shaking her pretty pink head. "This has to be a record."

Father's face was pondering as he chewed a slice of toast. "Why would anyone bring a match forward at this time of year? It doesn't make sense."

"I don't know," Daisy said, "but they did."

"A day's notice isn't much, either."

"Well, all I know is the kick-off is at half-past nine instead of half-past ten."

"At least it's a home match," Darwin said.

"Well," Dad said, standing up and brushing crumbs from his beard. "I just need to do one or two things…"

"Can you check Chutney first, Dad? To see if she'll start?" Daisy asked.

"Oh, she'll start. No worries. I put a blanket on her bonnet last night."

"You mean that blanket there?" Declan said.

Father looked at the blanket by the back door.

"Yes! That one!" he said and laughed. "Oh well, I'm sure she'll be fine."

"And I want to check *Leda's Lament* while the light is good. I wasn't happy with her bottom last night," Mum added.

Then Declan said, "I just want to test the new ladder to my treehouse..."

And Darwin said, "And I'll get my knitting..."

"Please make sure you're all back by nine o'clock," Daisy told them in a firm manner. "We must get to the cup match on time."

"Of course," everyone said.

Soon there was only me and Daisy in the kitchen. "Daisy," I asked her, "what do you think of the Callum Kirton situation? One Valentine card or two?"

Daisy did not reply. She took a piece of paper from her fleece pocket, glanced at it, then put it back. "Water bottles next," she said, which did not answer my question.

At nine o'clock Daisy was pacing up and down,

and I had decided two Valentine cards for Callum and one for Ellie. I would make them myself, using the glorious new felt pens Santa had brought me at Christmas.

"Right! That's *it*!" Daisy said, making me jump. Then she disappeared. By ten past nine everyone was back in the kitchen, Mum with a paintbrush in her hand, Dad with a big book called *Restoring Historical Buildings*, Declan sucking a cut on his hand and Darwin with his knitting.

"Time to go," Daisy said.

But then the phone rang. "I'll get that," Mother said.

"It'll be Granny," Daisy told her.

"So it will," Mother replied. "Do you want to take it, sweetheart?"

"Yes, yes," Daisy said, shooing us all out of the door. "I'll be one second. You guys go and get into Chutney."

"Daisy's very bossy these days," Darwin said to Declan as I followed them out.

☆ ☆ ☆

It was a frosty morning with watery yellow sunshine making everything sparkle in a highly beautiful and splendid way, especially Chutney. "She looks like a giant iced doughnut," Darwin said.

Sadly, despite her beauty, she would not start. I glanced at Daisy, expecting to see her face a bit blubby, but her profile was as calm as a pond.

"Sorry, girls. She needs a new battery," Father told us. "You'll have to miss the match today."

Just then something very strange happened. It was a miracle, probably. A minibus pulled into the driveway. A tall man with a turban and a dark beard even bushier than Father's got out. "Lornton?" he asked.

"That's us!" Daisy said with a leap and a bound over to him.

Something even more strange happened when he dropped us off. The match hadn't even started. It turned out it didn't begin until half-past ten after all. How peculiar!

☆ ☆ ☆

"OK, let's have you warming up. Once round the field, girls," Katie called out, and we all trotted round like ponies.

"I've hardly ever done this bit before," I said to Daisy.

"Me neither."

"It's good, isn't it? I can see all the cobwebs on the hedges."

Then we had a gather round. Hannah did the chatter for this part. "Right, girls," she said, "it's quite a special one today. As you know, if we win this we go top. Lose, and Furnston do. Of course it's not the end of the world if we do lose…"

"Want to bet!" Megan laughed.

Hannah wagged her finger at her, then continued, "But if we win it will give us an advantage going into the final match. It won't be easy, though. The Diamonds have had a women's team affiliated to the Furnston Brewery for years; they're well respected. When the Parrs play them we always know we're going to have a tough game, and the Diamonds junior squads are no different. So ... out of respect ... we're going to play the diamond formation..."

She then showed us all a mathsy diagram on her clippyboard and started talking – but then I remembered *our* clippyboard, because Daisy was meant to be making notes for the report. "Did you bring our clippyboard?" I whispered to her, but she didn't answer so I had to ask louder, and she frowned at me and shook her head and said shush. So I just thought, fine, be like that and sucked my hair.

"OK, I'll have Hols and Lucy at the back; Gem, Nika and JJ in the middle; and Eve up front to start. Remember, if you're not on the ball, fall back to help out in defence. Good luck, Parsnips!"

Then we did this cuddle thing where we all put our arms round each other's shoulders like we were doing a big whisper about someone and Meganini said, "Can we do this?" and everyone shouted, "Yes, we can!"

Daisy, Amy, Petra, Tabinda and me waited by the bottles for our turn. I wanted to link arms with Daisy, or do our clapping song, but she said she couldn't because she had to concentrate and she walked away from me and went to stand all by herself. So I watched on my own, but no one put a goal in the netty-box, which meant I couldn't do my aeroplane.

When the lady stoppy-starter blew her whistle for a tea break, everyone was so excited, even though it was nought–zero. "Wonderful stuff! You are playing brilliantly!" Hannah told us all.

"But you all need to play out wide more; use the wings," Katie added.

Then Hannah began the swaps. I like this bit and I stood nice and straight and quiet so she might pick me. "OK, Nika, you have a rest now; Tabinda, you go and hold that central midfield position. Amy, you go on for JJ … and…" She paused and looked at me. "Dyl, you can go on for Holly."

Standing nice and still worked! "Super!" I said.

"She'll never keep up with their number 10…" Holly began.

"She'll be fine."

Holly scowled and stomped off to talk to her father, who is a man of medium height, no beard and a tummy that looks like the dome of St Paul's Cathedral.

My twin gave me a huge hug and said, "Good luck."

I was doing very well indeed until I got confused. One second we were going one way, then the next another. My legs were galloping like all the king's horses and all the king's men and there was a lot of shouting. It was coming from many places and I didn't know who to listen to and my head felt full and fuzzy.

"Keep your eye on the ball, Dylan!" someone shouted. I turned round and couldn't believe it – the ball was coming straight at me!

"Clear it, Dylan! Clear it!" another voice yelled.

I tried. I kicked it hard – but it hit a Diamond on her stripy socks and bounced straight back at me, so I thought I'd try another direction and this time I twisted, kicked and whacked it. The ball zoomed as fast as a hare and even though Meganini stuck her boot out, my ball still went under her leg and into the netty-box. The Diamond girls were cheering and high-fiving each other and all the Parsnips were looking at me in disbelievingness.

Then the whistle blew and Hannah was waving at me. "You come off now, Dyl," she said, and Jenny-Jane came running on, but she didn't tig my hand or anything.

Hannah patted my shoulder when I walked over to the toothpaste track. "Don't worry about the own goal," she told me. "These things happen, even to the pros."

"Is an own goal bad?" I asked.

"Well, it's not brilliant," she said.

Even though Hannah smiled when she said it and didn't look one bit mad or anything, my tummy felt a bit churny, so I went to join my beloved twin and she gave me a hug and explained about the own goal still counting.

There were no more goals by the end so that meant it was one–nil to the Diamonds, who shouted, "Three cheers for the Parsnips! Hip-hip-hooray…" And then Meganini shouted, "Three cheers for Furnston!" and all my teamies did hip-hip-hooray. I liked that bit because it's what girls in Mrs Enid Blyton's wonderful books about Malory Towers would do, but Holly gave me a sour-lemon look when I shouted too loud and my stomach felt churny again.

6

*In which **Daisy McNeil** tells you about her granny's*

tactics and her eventful time at training

Mum and Dad waited until Sunday morning to grill me. They caught me alone in the kitchen just as I was going to take the biscuit tin upstairs for Dylan and me. "So let me get this straight," Mum said, yanking the tin away from me and setting it down on the table. "It wasn't Hannah on the phone on Friday but your granny, and the match didn't start at half-nine but at half-ten?"

"Yep," I replied.

"And Granny paid for the minibus weeks ago?" Dad asked.

"Yep. She was thinking ahead."

Mum began pacing up and down the kitchen floor. "I'm not happy. I'm not happy with this at all!" She went over to the sink and started banging dishes around. "Jim, you're going to have to talk to Susan. This is getting beyond a joke now…"

"I know, I know," said Dad, tugging at his beard.

"Don't tell Granny off. She was only trying to help," I said.

"Help!" Mum fumed.

"It was an important match. I had to make sure we got there on time."

Mum stopped pacing and looked at me. Her eyes were more worried than angry. "Look, Daisy, I have to tell you I'm thinking football might not be such a good thing for you to do after all."

"Why?"

"Well, I approved at first, because girls playing football is excellent for gender equality, but I think it's making you anxious and competitive."

"It's not!"

Dad joined in then. "I'm totally with your mum

on this, Daisy. Look at what happened yesterday. Nothing's so urgent that you have to lie to us."

"It wasn't a lie; it was a tactic. Granny says without tactics you're doomed in this family."

"Did she, now…" Dad said in a low voice.

"She did. She says the male McNeils are notoriously disorganized and would be late for their own funerals."

Mum tutted and Dad said, "Everybody's disorganized compared with your granny, Daisy. She ran the house like an army camp when I was little. I remember once we were packing for our summer holidays in January! No kidding. That's why I want my own family life to be more chilled out."

"Quite," Mum agreed.

I screwed up my face, remembering everything Granny had told me to say if Dad brought up the early packing story. "*And he will, Daisy. Trust me. He brings it up at every opportunity…*" I took a deep breath. "Well, there's a time to be chilled out and a time to be on time. And when you're part of a team, it's a time to be on time."

"Well, we were on time and you still didn't get to play!" Mum pointed out.

"That just shows you don't know anything about football," I said, snatching the biscuit tin and hurrying upstairs.

Mum and Dad didn't say anything again about alarm clocks and minibuses, but later that day a man from Mowborough Motors came out and fitted a new battery and some things called spark plugs in Chutney, and on Monday we were on time for school and on Tuesday we were on time for training.

Training is in Darwin and Declan's school sports hall now because of winter. I like having training there, because the hall is huge and I love the squeaky sound your trainers make when you run on the shiny floor. Today I didn't try to make the floor squeak, though, or shout louder to make the hall echo. I was too excited, because I'd written a report that would thrill Megan so much. I couldn't wait to hand it in at the end of training.

First we joined in a circle, doing stretches. I had Dylan on one side and Tabinda on the other.

"OK," Hannah said, standing opposite us, "space out and make wide circles with your arms. Like windmills."

"Ouch! Watch it!" I heard Holly say. Dylan was on her right and must have hit her.

"Can't help it! I live in a windmill. I'm an expert at windmill arms," Dylan told Holly.

"I'm glad you're an expert at *something*," Holly said in a mean way.

"She's talking about my own goal, isn't she?" Dylan asked me.

"I think so. We'd best keep away from her tonight," I told her. That's what dinner supervisors always tell us to do at school if someone's mean to us – though it's quite hard when you're supposed to be passing the ball to them in a three.

By the end of training Dylan had only bumped into Holly once more, and that was when we were tidying up. Dylan had put a ball up her T-shirt, pretending she was having a baby, and she swung round and knocked Holly's arm. Holly didn't say anything this time; she just walked off in a huff.

When we'd warmed down, Hannah clapped her hands and said, "Good session, girls. Awesome. You work harder than half the senior team!"

"Sad but true!" Katie laughed.

Then we went to sit on the benches for a talk. I tried to sit near Megan so I could tell her about the report, but Megan's highly popular and I could only manage four places to her left.

"So, we've got a league match against the Cuddlethorpe Tigers on Saturday…" Hannah began.

She talked about that for a bit, then Megan put her hand up. "Can we talk about the cup run now?" and I thought, "Yes, please," and half stood up to go and get my epic report, but Megan was pulling something out of her rucksack so I sat down again.

"It's just I've got the updated table here. I printed one off for Daisy and Dylan with the match report, and I did a few spares if anybody wants one."

"OK," Hannah said.

As Megan began handing sheets round I felt a little bit put out. So she'd printed out Hannah's report already, before I'd even had a chance to show her mine. "Here you go!" Megan said with a big smile on her face as she reached us. "Saved you a job!"

"But Daisy's…" Dylan began, but I nudged her to stop because I had just realized something. The way Megan had pulled those reports out of her bag was just how Granny had pulled the box of Tetley tea bags out of her handbag that time. Megan hadn't printed out those match reports because she was super-thoughtful. She'd been thinking ahead, just like Granny did! So that was why she'd been calm and kind about the Greenbow game and unruffled about us only being there for half of the match against Lutton Ash Angels.

Megan wasn't bothered one bit whether we delivered our reports on the cup run! She had Hannah's reports anyway!

I felt a lump come into my throat the size of a coconut and quickly dropped my head to pretend I was engrossed in the table. Around me, people began muttering. Here's the table, in case you want to mutter too:

Team	P	W	D	L	F	A	Pts
Furnston Diamonds	3	3	0	0	12	1	9
Parrs U11s	3	2	0	1	10	3	6
Greenbow United Girls	3	1	1	1	9	8	4
Misslecott Goldstars	3	0	2	1	5	10	2
Lutton Ash Angels	4	0	1	3	6	20	1

"We'll never catch Furnston!" Holly groaned.

"We're still second," Eve pointed out. "Always look on the bright side."

"It's not disastrous. Furnston play Greenbow next and we play Misslecott, so if Greenbow beat

Furnston and we beat Misslecott, we'll both be on nine points..." Megan noticed.

"Then it's down to goal difference! Cool!" Eve said.

"Not going to happen," Holly said. "No chance."

I wanted to keep listening, but Dylan cupped her hand over my ear and started whispering, "Why didn't you tell Megan about your report?"

I pulled away from her and shrugged. "It doesn't matter."

Dylan tapped Hannah's website report. "It does. Yours is heaps better. Hannah really uses the word 'awesome' too much, you know."

"What was that?" Hannah asked, glancing towards us when she heard her name.

Luckily we didn't have to explain, because Holly had her hand up and wanted her attention. "Hannah, can I ask you something?" she said, her mouth small and tight as a winkle. Something in the way she glowered at me and Dylan when she asked made my heart beat faster.

"Sure, Holly. What is it?"

"I was just wondering why you let Dylan play on Saturday?"

Suddenly all the chattering on the benches stopped. "What do you mean?" Hannah asked.

Holly, knowing everyone was listening, hesitated, then sat up straight. "Well, when it's an important match my dad says you should always field your strongest team, unless there's an injury."

Hannah looked quite cross. "I'm afraid your dad's doing what a lot of parents tend to do. He's comparing our level to a professional level."

"At *any* level, Dad says. Bringing Dylan on cost us the game. That own goal was totally avoidable."

Katie frowned. "Anyone can score an own goal, Holly. It's par for the course in defence. At *any* level."

Holly's face had turned pink but she wouldn't back down. "I know that, but ... well, Dylan wasn't even *trying* to clear it. She turned round and had a shot!" Holly glared at Dylan. "Admit it, you did it on purpose, didn't you?"

I felt Dylan hitch closer to me and I reached for her hand. There was a horrible silence. Nobody said a word. Nobody. I felt the back of my legs prickle, because I knew then that they all agreed with Holly.

Only Hannah stood up for us. "Well, you must remember the twins are the youngest…"

"That's not why they do it, though, is it? I know loads of Year Threes who act more maturely than they do…" Holly looked straight at Dylan. "I'm not trying to be mean, Dylan, honest I'm not, but even tonight you mucked about instead of trying harder to make up for Saturday. You just don't seem to be bothered."

"Bothered! Hovered!" said Dylan in a silly voice.

"See?" Holly said, throwing her hands up in despair.

My hands began to tremble. Granny had warned me this time would come. The time when we'd have to explain. "And it'll be better coming from you than from your sister," she'd said. I took a deep breath and stood up. Dylan leapt up beside me and I held onto her fast, to show I was still on her side and that I needed her. "May I say something?" I asked.

"Course you can," Hannah said.

"I just want to say that ... I just want to say that Holly's right."

"Am I?" Holly asked, looking up with a surprised expression on her face.

I nodded. "Yes, you are. Dylan does mess about sometimes. I do too, but usually it's because we get muddled, and when we get muddled" – I paused, trying to remember how Granny had explained it to me over Christmas – "instead of being sensible and *telling* people we're muddled ... we act giddy to hide it..."

"That's so true! We do!" Dylan exclaimed.

"And that annoys people..."

"My friend Ellie tells me I'm annoying every day," Dylan said proudly.

A few people laughed and that broke the tension in the room.

"But we don't do it on purpose," I continued. "Granny says we're dyslexic and probably a bit hyperactive, but Mum doesn't want us being labelled like cheese so we don't know for definite *what* we are." I focused on Holly. "But we do both love football and we *are* trying ... especially on the time thing..." I turned to Megan. "And I know you think we're rubbish at remembering the reports, too, but I did do a proper one this time – one that Leicester Ladies would understand. It's in my bag."

Megan bit her lip. "I'm sorry, Daisy."

"I'm sorry too," Holly said. Her face had turned redder than a bowl of ripe strawberries. "I thought you were just messing about because that's what you did. I didn't ... I didn't know there was a reason for it. My friend Lauren's dyslexic. She has special blue glasses to help her read and everything..."

"We might *not* be dyslexic. We're very good readers, but we do have some things that match the dyslexia thing, like the twaddly spelling and not being able to take in loads of instructions all at once. It's only what my granny thinks, though…" I said quickly because behind me I could hear the door opening and closing as parents came to collect us. Mum would not be happy if she overheard. "Anyway, that's why we mess up," I said in a whisper. "If you want us to drop out of the team, we will. We might be dropping out anyway, because of our self-esteem damage."

"Oh, you can't drop out!" Tabinda cried. "It wouldn't be the same without you! Who would lead the singing?"

"Too right! We need the psycho twins on the team!" Eve laughed. "We're the envy of the league!"

"Every team should have some!" Petra nodded.

Then, before we knew what was happening, every Parsnip but one jumped off the benches and piled round us, hugging us and rubbing our heads with their knuckles. As I came up for air, I saw only Holly

had held back. "Come on, Hollybolly Woolcock!"
I called out. "Party time."

Her face broke into a grin. "OK!" she said, and
joined the best group hug ever.

"These girls!" Hannah said to Katie. "What are
they like?"

*In which **Miss Dylan McNeil** explains the wing game*

using her best vocabulary (and football words always

found in dictionaries)

I begin this part once upon a time at eight-o-ten on Saturday 2 March. I leapt out of bed, fully dressed as a Parsnip, put on my trainers, ran to the bathroom for a wee and a wash and then went downstairs in a highly unrushed manner for breakfast.

At the table were Daisy and my granny. Granny had come all the way from Dundeeland to watch us play the Misslecott Goldstars that morning. When Daisy told her that we had to win by several goals and Furnston had to lose to Greenbow by not so many goals so that we could get to the final of the

Nettie Honeyball Cup, she booked her train ticket straight away and said she wouldn't miss this match for the world.

"Well done," Granny said to me as I arrived and took my place round the cereal boxes we had set out the night before. "Five minutes early."

"Och aye the noo!" I replied.

"So you're all set?"

"I am. I don't know about my twin."

"I am." Daisy nodded. "But I feel nervous."

"Good!" Granny said, dipping her Tetley tea bag in and out of her mug. "So you should. Ah! Here come the boys."

Darwin and Declan clattered down the stairs, making Sedge jump up in excitement and Pickle dart under my chair. "Two-four-six-eight, who do we appreciate..." they called, waving Declan's knitted red and white scarves in the air.

"Not the King, not the Queen, but the Parsnips football team!" Granny laughed, getting out her Dundee FC scarf.

A few minutes later we were joined for toast and jam by our beloved parents, and at nine-o-ten precisely there was a tooting outside our windmill home – the minibus had arrived!

"My treat," Granny said.

"That's so kind of you," Mother replied – and she meant it, because Chutney's heating was not working and the morning was not a fine one.

At nine-o-fifty we arrived at the Misslecott Goldstars ground. "Do you think they'll be wearing gold stars?" I asked Daisy as Granny paid the taxi driver, who was called Rajinder and supported Derby County. (So does my future husband, Callum Kirton, by the way.)

"I don't know," Daisy said, taking deep breaths.

As we walked across the car park towards the Goldstars playing field I felt my tummy swishing with Coco Pops and pride. Lots of players had brought their mums and dads with them, person reading this, but no one had twin brothers and a Scottish granny too. Ha!

I didn't brag about it, though. I had to concentrate. Hannah gathered us all round for the team talk. "Right, girls. No speeches from Katie or me today, we just want you to go out there and enjoy yourselves. OK?"

"OK!" we all chorused.

"Wicked! Right, Eve … you begin up front … Gemma … central midfield. Amy, right wing, and Dylan…" Hannah paused and nodded towards me in a solemn manner. "You know what to do?"

I nodded.

I did know, because ever since what I call "the incredible incident in the sports hall" my life as a footballer has become full of joy and happiness. What happened was this. The following week at training, Hannah and Katie took Daisy and me to one side and asked us what feelings we had when we played. I told them about my fuzzy head and they nodded. "What we'll do is just give you a few instructions at a time from now on," they said, "and if you get confused by anything – anything at all – just let us know."

And that's what I do.

"So tell me where you are going to stand," Hannah now said to me.

"I am going to stand on the opposite side from Amy," I said in a proud way.

"And what are you going to do?"

"I am going to play the wing game."

"Good girl!" Katie beamed. "Off you go."

I ran to take up my position on the correct side of the pitch.

Then the referee blew her whistle and we began the match. The crowd cheered but I blocked them out. I admit I had a quick peepo at the Goldstars to see if they were wearing gold stars, but they weren't. They were wearing gold-coloured tops and green shorts but nothing star-shaped.

Apart from that I kept my eye on where the ball was all the time, while staying in the channel inside the touchline. In case you don't know, person reading this, the channel is like a cycle path for footballers called McNeil. It is what I used to call a toothpaste track but is really the bit parallel to the touchline. The *touchline.* I am highly expert on football words now, because Megan and Petra spend whole lunchtimes at school teaching them to me. They have been kind and helpful, like Hannah and Katie. All the team has.

It makes Mum splendidly joyous. She doesn't think football is too competitive any more. In fact she tells everyone how playing sport is probably the best thing that could have happened for our co-ordination and self-confidence. She says it just goes to show kids don't need tests to improve their skills; they just need kindness and patience. All in all, Daisy revealing our muddledness that day turned out to be a highly good thing.

Anyway, Megan had a goal kick. She kicked the ball hard and low towards Petra on her left, who immediately passed it to me because she could see I was free and that was the rule. As soon as the ball came to me, I put my foot on top of it to stop it going out, then ran with it along the channel, to just past the halfway line. Nobody shouted "Man on" and I couldn't see any alien boots near by, so I kept going, then slowed down enough to look round, saw Jenny-Jane was unmarked and passed the ball to her using the inside of my foot. That was my bit done. It is called the wing game. I am quite the expert on the wing game. That's because I have practised it three million seven hundred times.

After I had passed, I watched, but in a highly alert way because I have to be prepared for if we lose possession (that means if the other team gets it off us, person reading this) and the ball comes back towards me.

It didn't, though. Jenny-Jane was too tough! She drizzle-drazzled the ball right past one defender and across towards the box, but then, instead of passing to Eve, who was calling for it, Jenny-Jane tried to run round a second defender – but this one was a big girl and she blocked Jenny-Jane's shot and the ball went out for a throw-in.

Jenny-Jane looked a bit skulky, but fell back into position while Nika took the throw-in. The ball landed right at Jenny-Jane's feet and this time she passed immediately to Eve, who was on the edge of the box. Eve tapped it neatly to Gemma, who splunked it into the back of the net. Goal! One–nil to us! Then I did my aeroplane, because I'm still allowed to do those when we score, as long as I stay on the pitch.

After I'd played the wing game loads more, Hannah called me off to swap with Tabinda. Tabinda gave me a high five as she came on and I high-fived her back. "Nice one," she told me.

"Thank you," I said, my head growing bigger by the second. I grinned and put my thumbs up at my beloved family and they clapped me and swayed from side to side with their scarves outstretched. I had a swiggle of water and went for a chat with Lucy, who hadn't played yet.

"You were amazing," she told me.

"I know," I said. "I'm highly awesome."

☆ ☆ ☆

At half-time it was still one–nil.

"Come on, you guys up front. This lot are pants! We need more goals!" Megan said as we gathered round our pile of bags and bottles.

"No? Do we really?" Eve replied.

"Yeah. That's how you win, apparently," Lucy added.

"Well, I wish someone had told me!" Eve said, slapping her forehead.

I laughed then, because my teamies are so funny sometimes, but I didn't laugh so much that I got hiccups or that they'd stare at me.

Hannah strolled across to us. "Well, folks, my spies tell me that in the other match Greenbow are winning one–nil."

"One–nil! Dream score! Yes!" Megan said and punched the air.

"So just keep doing what you're doing and the goals will come. Remember to move *to* the ball and be on your toes, ready to react all the time.

Misslecott aren't particularly skilful but they've got some big players…"

"No kidding!" Katie said to Hannah. "That number 31 could fit Daisy in her pocket!"

"She'd have to catch me first!" Daisy said.

"That's the spirit!" Hannah said, ruffling Daisy's hair. "Right … let's confuse the opposition and have both twins on the wings at the same time… Dylan left, Daisy right…"

"Jolly good!" I said and gave Daisy a hug.

I think my teamies are very good listeners, because almost as soon as the referee blew his whistle Eve scored a goal. Her mum and brothers were jumping up and cheering so much, although not quite as much as my beloved parents, brothers and granny. McNeils are highly excellent cheerers.

Everything felt so tense and exciting. My tummy bubbled as if it were Christmas Eve and Halloween at the same time. That was until the defender who was marking Daisy barged into her and sent her flying. I let out an angry yell and forgot all about staying in position and pelted straight across the field. Katie was already helping Daisy hobble off. I was breathing very hard and had to count to ten fast. "Do that again and I'll be very cross!" I told the girl, who had a mean look on her face. Well, I think she did. She was so tall I could only see as far as her hairy nostrils.

"Ooooh, I'm scared." The girl smirked.

"You will be," a voice next to me said. I turned – and there was my friend Holly, squaring up to the big girl. Holly always leaps to our defence now if anybody has a go at us in matches. She's been awfully kind since that time in the sports hall.

"Come on, then," the girl dared Holly. My heart was pounding so much. This never happens in Malory Towers!

"All right! All right!" the referee said, pushing them apart. "Time out!"

The Goldstars coach came running up then and swapped the big girl over for a medium-sized one with a kinder face, and the referee gave us a direct free kick – but I wouldn't budge until I knew Daisy was OK. Mum, Dad and Granny were already bending over her, checking her ankle.

"Keep playing, Dylan," Daisy called to me. "I'm fine."

"Come on, Dylan," Gemma said, putting her arm round my shoulder and leading me away. "Let's score another one. For Daisy."

And that's what we did! Nika took the free kick. It looped above all the Goldstars players' heads, bounced off the crossbar and into Tabinda, who chested it down, aimed and shot straight at the goalie. The goalie tried to kick it away, but she messed up and it only went as far as Gemma. Ping! Three–nil!

That was the final score. As soon as we had hip-hip-hoorayed I dashed over to my twin to see how she was. Her face was crest-dropped. "Are you still so severely injured?" I asked her.

"No. It's just that we're out of the cup. I heard Katie tell Hannah that Furnston drew one-all with Greenbow so they're through to the final by one point."

"Oh." I sighed. But then I remembered what Eve had said at training about looking on the bright side. "Well, at least we don't have to write up any more reports."

"We haven't done one yet!" Daisy laughed.

"That's true." I smiled, remembering that even our last one hadn't been used, because when Daisy had gone to get it from her bag to show Megan, she discovered she had put in one of Darwin's knitting patterns by mistake. Worse, when we got home we found out Mum had seen the report on the table and used it in a collage.

"I give up," Daisy had said.

The news that we were out of the cup meant everybody looked crest-dropped. "Never mind, girls. We came second. And there's always next year," Hannah told us.

"I suppose," Megan said. She sighed. "I guess we'll just have to concentrate on the league."

"As they say." Katie laughed.

"Well, before you all disappear, there's one more piece of business to attend to," Hannah announced and began flummaging in her sports bag.

"Now," she said, pulling out the golden globey, "how to decide? You were all tremendous, but two of you were especially outstanding. Our twins on the wings, Dylan and Daisy…" Daisy's jaw dropped and I did a little squeal and stopped breathing. We'd never won the golden globey before!

"Yay!" Megan said, giving us a clap.

"But I've only got one trophy," Hannah said, her voice pretending to be all sad.

"They can share it. They're twins; they're used to that," Tabinda said.

"No way!" Hannah declared and flummaged in her bag again. "Of course they're not sharing! They deserve a trophy each!"

She had been teasing us! Oh! When she

presented us with the golden globeys I had wet eyes and Mum and Dad and Granny had wet eyes, and Darwin had wet eyes and Declan didn't but he had pleased eyes, and Daisy had dry eyes but they were so wide they looked like blue marbles.

And that's how the cup run ended.

Final Whistle

Well, person reading this, we hope you enjoyed hearing about our adventures in the Nettie Honeyball Cup run. We were especially pleased we won a golden globey each because it meant we had a happy ending. Mrs Enid Blyton would have approved of that!

The Grove Belles won the cup in the end. They beat Furnston Diamonds four-one. We think it is a shame because the Grove Belles have won the Nettie Honeyball Cup every year since it began in 2002. They should give someone else a go, if you want our opinion.

Next, Holly is going to tell you about what happened at the

end of our first season and the big presentation evening. She is a sensible person, so we know her story will not be upside-down or in Elvish. It will be highly interesting and splendid, though.

Well, goodbye! Goodbye from Dylan and Daisy, Darwin and Declan, Luna and Jim. Goodbye from our beloved Scottish granny. Goodbye from Sedge, Pickle and Beetroot and our camper van, Chutney.

Goodbye till next time. We'll meet you again soon.

Lots of love
Dylan and Daisy McNeil

xxxxxxxxxxxxxxxxxxxxxxxxxxxxxxxxxxxxxxx

More from Nadia FC

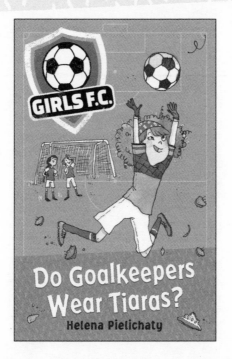

Megan is desperate to be picked for her school football team. She tries everything to get the coach to notice her (even wearing a tiara) but nothing seems to work. That's when she has her big idea: she could start her own team. An all-girls team!

Now she just needs a pitch, a coach — oh, and at least ten other players...

More from Girls F.C.

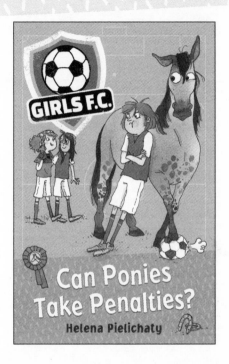

Petra can't wait to play in her first football tournament. While she's not exactly the best defender, it's great spending time with her friend Megan — the team captain.

But the big match clashes with her sister's show-jumping event and, as usual, Charlotte (and her dumb ponies) are her mum's number one priority...

More from Girls F.C.

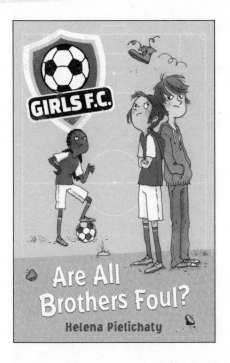

Lucy loves football — it's what she lives
for. But her older brother Harry has been
acting up since their parents' divorce
and his moods are making things tense.

Lucy tries to be the peacemaker, but when
Harry's bad behaviour spills over into her
football she knows it's time to make a stand.